Hornpipe Humoresque

A Nautical Extravaganza for Organ
by Noel Rawsthorne

We hope you enjoy the music in this book.
Further copies of this and our many other books are available
from your local music shop or Christian bookshop.

In case of difficulty, please contact the publisher direct by writing to:

The Sales Department
KEVIN MAYHEW LTD
Rattlesden
Bury St Edmunds
Suffolk IP30 0SZ

Phone 01449 737978
Fax 01449 737834

Please ask for our complete catalogue of outstanding Church Music.

Front Cover: *Naval Manoeuvres* by Edwin Roberts (1840-1917).
Reproduced by kind permission of Fine Art Photographic, London.

Cover designed by Graham Johnstone and Veronica Ward

First published in Great Britain in 1995 by Kevin Mayhew Ltd

ISBN 0 86209 689 8
Catalogue No: 1400059

Music Editor: Donald Thomson
Music setting by Daniel Kelly

Printed and bound in Great Britain

HORNPIPE HUMORESQUE

Noel Rawsthorne (*b.*1929)

Più mosso (♩ = 84)

8'4'2' Flutes

16'8' Flutes

* With apologies to J S Bach

cresc. poco a poco

Gt.*mf* (*2nd time* *f*)

simile

1. 2.

ff † 8'4' Tubas

* *With apologies to Vivaldi*

† *With apologies to Arne*

Grandioso

rall. poco a poco   a tempo

ff

simile

32'16'8' Reeds

With apologies to Widor